T0064493

EAT LIVE
and
LET'S LIVE

Neither a Vegetarian nor an Advocate

Rev Ami

authorHOUSE®

AuthorHouse™
1663 Liberty Drive
Bloomington, IN 47403
www.authorhouse.com
Phone: 1 (800) 839-8640

Published by AuthorHouse   08/21/2015

ISBN: 978-1-5049-3009-3 (sc)
ISBN: 978-1-5049-3008-6 (e)

PREFACE

And God said, "see! I *have given* you every herb that yields seed…"

If there is any human being out there listening, I have been given the privilege to speak up and speak out. I am a plant. I am speaking on behave of the other plants on earth. I hope you are giving me your attention as I clarify few things.

"Could it be because you don't see red liquid gushing out of plants like animals and human blood when they are bleeding, or could it be because you don't observe struggling, resisting movement by plants like other living things put up when their lives are at stake? Please do not draw wrong conclusions that we don't feel pain that's why we don't run away from predators. Unfortunately we are by nature restricted to one spot unless removed. Get to work, get busy, do more research, you may discover our nervous system is very complex. I wish you would admit that humans are selfish. You cause other beings to suffer and die for you to live. My blood is not red but clear liquid; some are red, some are green, some are smeared in other colors and textures. On the whole, we have one thing in common: our bloods come in liquid forms like animals and your red blood. See a picture of my kin chopped down and bleeding to death…do you see it, ugly and pitifully castrated before your eyes."

"Plants may not talk, nor do leaves cry in your language. No one can really hear their cry nor feel their pain. This Author portrays us as animals so that humans could visualize us as living things; so that humans that consumed them may realized that just as they feel pain if cut, so do plants; as humans bleed when cut, so do plants; so that the Animal Advocates, the Vegetarians may also realized that these plants are maimed, destroyed, killed as they are consumed; that they may know as they cry out for the animals – stand against animal cruelty, that they

(Advocates) are as guilty by consuming these vegetables. You have destroyed your reputation. Again, both animals and vegetables are Living Things. Both bleed if cut. Take a look at the defense mechanism of tropical plant such as Mimosa Pudica below:

It's so sensitive, so famously resilient to touch. Touch it, the leaves fold in resistance, but not enough to escape human brutal hands that pluck its beautiful flowers. S-s-h! Listen, the vegetables are screaming, somebody is cutting them. Both die if killed. Hush! Look, someone is cooking them. So stop complaining and criticizing, appreciate what nature has rightfully given to you. If anything must live, it must eat. So hush, Eat and live!

SPECIAL THANKS

To my daughter, Faith, who, is a huge support and the inspiration behind this <u>Book.</u> She is a Go-getter. I suspended writing this Book for almost four years. When I announced that I've resumed writing and must complete it, Faith made sure I'm reminded of the task when I seemed to have abandoned writing. I love you!

But my greatest strength came from unfeigned faith and dependence on my strong and Almighty God. Bravo!

SPECIAL NOTES AND DISCLAIMER

The works of this Book is partly based on true life events. Partly it is fictitious due to arrangement in characters, times and some places of occurrence. The names of some characters had been altered. In no means is it the intention of the Author to use someone's name dead or alive in true representation of their persons, personalities and profiles. The Author's name is intentionally used to identify some degree of truth.

It was a beautiful Sunday afternoon in June. The temperature was in the 60's, cold, but sunny. Family was dinning out in an area restaurant.

"After today, I'm not eating meat anymore," Faith said.

"May I ask why?" her mother asked at the table as they ate.

"It's her New Year's resolution, I supposed," the father cut in without giving the daughter a chance to answer the mother.

"I want to be a *vegetarian,*" Faith finally answered.

"For how long do you intend to keep it that way?" the father asked.

"For the rest of my life," Faith sounded conclusive with her new intentions.

Faith is 18 years old. She likes to throw challenges on herself from time to time. She does not attached much consideration as to how many huddles each challenge may have or what effort is required to accomplish each challenge. To become a vegetarian is a good example of such challenges. What prompted this idea was not specified as she attempted to clarify her reasons to the entire family members. She refuted it is human cruelty to animals. *It is neither a dislike of meat consumption nor is she an animal advocate.* However, she does feel sorry for the animals as they are being slaughtered to provide meals to the humans. She also leans on the health effect caused by excess meat consumption. As to the burden of sacrifices animals carry in order to sustain man's life, the father pointed Faith in the direction of the right and privilege God gave to man.

"It's in the Bible, in Genesis….." the father said as he pulled out of the restaurant's parking lot heading home.

"I knew you were going to say that," Faith jumped in giggling before her father could finish quoting the portion of the Bible. It was obvious this was not the first time this line of reasoning had taken place.

"You're right," the father replied. "God gave man the permission to eat meat and plants. Genesis chapter 1:26-29. Get the Bible," he directed. Faith quickly reached for the Bible that is always kept in the van. She began to read…..

"You see," he affirmed. "The Creator provided a prescriptive diet to human kind. In order for one thing to live, another has to die. A seed that is planted dies first, then, germinates. Soldiers give their lives to defend a nation. Jesus gave his life for our soul's salvation as per our Christian belief. Animals and plants must die in order for humans to live," he concluded.

The father has tremendous knowledge about the Bible. He has served as clergy, held pastorate position in the church. The manner in which he spoke showed Christian pride and revolt against some people's false interpretation of the scriptures to suit their lifestyles. This strikes a very modern note on how people view religion.

"I got to tell you this," he picked up conversation after a brief silence. "There is so much prejudice among preferred vegetarians against meat consumers. I watched my co-workers arguing almost near fist fight as to how wrong it is to kill animals for food – clear battery and ignorance. The animal-rights activists picket at meat- serving- restaurants. Meat processing factories are constant target and scrutiny."

Years ago, this Author witnessed an advocate groups, Solidarity Front for Animal Rights (SOFAR) protested the way chickens are slaughtered for consumption at the fast-food chain Restaurants. The group on a bright sunny Saturday afternoon picket right in a shopping mall parking lot to vent their anger. A public food event was held on the lot with restaurants and fast-food chains represented.

Members of SOFAR carried signs with pictures of 'bloody chicken held over pot of boiling water,' 'unhappy chickens.' Placards were displayed with several inscriptions like: 'free the chickens,' 'stop cruelty to chickens and their buddies.' Their scheme included a gigantic chicken balloon with no feathers placed on a pick-up truck. The chicken carried a message on its beak: "To all CHICKEN & ANIMAL serving Restaurants – Got the PICTURE!" Few of the organizers actually had on chicken costumes. The scene created mixed feelings as event patrons made joking remarks about the pictures and some remarks either in support of the protesters or the restaurants. The person standing next to me shouted, "Sorry, I love you chickens." SOFAR group must have been disappointed because their showdown was aimed to discourage and sway the people from patronizing these restaurants and most importantly resolved to be vegetarians. Sadly they did not make much impact as majority in the crowd were still busy buying meals at the stands. Some patrons did not even care the groups were there.

What's the big deal or so idealistic the way chicken or any animal for that matter should be killed. Either method used, they are still being put to death. A ridiculous 'humanely' slaughtering suggestion by SOFAR ring leader is to create a controlled environmental killing by way of shorting off or limiting supply of oxygen to chickens in transit to their final destinations of doom. What would this method do, let the chicken to die slowly. That's a horrifying experiment. What should this method be coined - *Mercy Killings?*

May I ask, "Do SOFAR has realistic way vegetables and plants in general should be slaughter?" Their answer likely would be that plants do not have throats to be slit open. But be aware they are full of life and abstract consciousness if not full consciousness as animals do. Think! Please think again before you respond. There is no study yet in place to reveal plants are susceptible to pain as well as suffering – just use your imagination. I have never heard of 'cruelty-free food'. How about this, there are News reports on Television, online, social media about some animal-rights activists who dressed in all kinds of vegetables and plants species in attempt to persuade meat-eaters to be vegetarians. To some degree they've succeeded capturing the public attention but not necessarily successful converting them; rather they got captured for disturbing public peace. May I joined with the schools of thought that we should gear our efforts and energies in promoting health ideology, food safety, environmental challenges than fight a seemingly lost battle of using animals plight to try to stop some groups that harmoniously enjoy to eat meals prepared with animal meats and or animal products. Certain choices we make in life do not translate into being indifferent to equally important concerns and issues. Part of human problems can be identified in centuries of 'ABUSES' around us like child, spouse, animal and including human abuses well pronounced during slavery era even prevalent today.

WHAT Is WRONG WITH THESE PICTURES: MAR'TYRDOM – Trees on fire burnt alive! Martyrs!

"It is fascinating what manure compost is derived from. I'll tell you should you don't know," their father seemed to adjust his posture for this piece of information. "From solid waste, yes, solid waste from farm animals (excreta from livestock) excreta from human beings, decomposed animals including insects and crops…

"Whew!" Faith reacted.

"Ooh no!" Maxwell followed suit.

"Absolutely yes," the father fast tracked his tutoring. "Manure is generally great to fertilized the land especially soil for cultivating plants and vegetables. So, in order to grow and harvest best or succulent vegetables like lettuce, cucumbers, tomatoes, potatoes, celeries, cauliflowers, peppers, etc. for our appetites, animals are killed. Who are guilty? Is it the meat consumers who directly kill animals for food or some thoughtless vegetarians and animal advocates who indirectly support killing animals for the by-product to raise, protect their vegetables and crops in general."

"Both," all jumped for the same answer.

"Absolutely correct," the father again confirmed. "Another view of the matter is the ethical issue of using animals for medical experiment and research to benefit humans in time of illness or sickness. Should we, rather sanction the use of human beings for the medical purposes. It is really not a secret some unfortunate humans had paid the death price in the brutal hands of heartless people in this direction who do not have regards to or care less about human life. How should we honestly justify that? Shame! shame."

A brief silence ensued as they rode along till their attentions are caught by a seemingly large crowd.

"Look guys," Maxwell pointed at a group of people carrying signs at a local horse race course.

"They are picketing," Jeremiah clarified.

Maxwell and Jeremiah are Faith's brothers. Jeremiah is the oldest of the three.

"Those are animal *advocates,*" Jeremiah continued. "They are speaking for the circus animals," everyone laughed.

"The elephants can't protest like that with signs, the dogs also. All they could do is bark. You can shut them up with a piece of biscuit or beef in their mouths," Jeremiah joked but serious. "The cats, I'm afraid…"

"What cats," Maxwell cuts in not allowing the brother to finish. "I've never seen cats at any circus yet," he ended.

"I'm talking about the tigers, dummy," Jeremiah referring to his brother. Faith quipped.

"Don't call your brother dummy," mom interrupted. (Maxwell pushed Jeremiah) Jeremiah reacted causing a little squabble between them. This prompted the father to pull the vehicle to the road side.

"See! See! This is what I always talked about," he roared angrily. "Family disputes are not uncommon resulting in split relationships. Those animals are smarter than you and most of those advocates who think the animals are being abused in the process of training and putting on a show…"

"Dad," Jeremiah tried to call the father's attention on his remarks that 'animals are smarter' than them, but the father ignored him and continued.

"Poor grass," he snapped. He paused as if to change the topic.

"Check out the stunts those animals do performed. Direct the elephants to sit, they sit. Command them to go in circle, they obeyed. Have them to pose a salute, they amazed you. The tigers jump through rings of fire. The puppies have a bag full of tricks - well coordinated. If they are trained to carry signs in protest like the humans do, would probably learned," he concluded. Jeremiah and others started laughing forgetting about his intent to confront his father remarks made earlier. The father couldn't help but laugh too only to drive home his point by saying:

"Let's face it, the unnecessary personal attacks and criticism, the character assassinations and belief is causing more damages to our already divided society – over what? A choice to eat either meat, vegetable or both combined. As if that is not enough, the religious overviews as to who is right or who is wrong bring more confusion. God must be amused."

"Okay dad, you've made your point," Maxwell looked around as if seeking everyone's agreement on his intervention.

"All the creatures were created by God. Humans were given the privilege to use them for food. They all sustained human lives," Maxwell rested but not without an echo of

"Amen!" by Jeremiah spinning another round of laughter by everyone.

"Poor grass!" the father exclaimed again. "Look at how people walked all over them. Look at the advocates trampled mercilessly upon them. Can you hear them screaming? Do you see them struggling? Can't you hear their cries?" the father questions pointing to the grass at the race course. "Imagine the grass could move in protest to attack. I bet those so called advocates would be stampeding, running helter-skelter for their dear lives."

Everyone burst out laughing uncontrollably. "Imagine those grass could revolt like the story of the animals' revolution in ANIMAL FARM by George Orwell," he ended on a much serious note. "It's sad no one could see their agonizing tears," he looked pitiful. "It's sad no one could hear the plants voices in protest," his face looked soggy. "Who listens to them?" he paused, "Anyone?" He sighed.

"Days after the circus, the unlucky grass would withered and died after being senselessly walked upon, smashed, crushed by people's feet. If by chance they are timely sprayed with water, resuscitated, yet would go through the same ordeal over and over again while some are completely uprooted," he appeared exhausted and empty to paint a replica picture of the wearied grass. "It is true about the saying: 'when two elephants fight, it is the grass that suffers'," he grinned as he added, "they are unprotected. They are vulnerable to man's brutality…"

"Dad," Faith called the father. But he acted as if he did not hear her.

"The advocates are fanning themselves probably thinking they've done great justice standing up for the animals," the father indirectly vaunted.

"Da-a-d," Faith called again. The father turned, looked at her then looked away and about to continue with his narrative. But Faith acted quickly:

"Why don't you write a book about this, it will sell," she sounded certain but really an attempt to change the subject and terminated the father's enthusiasm on the topic.

"Let me tell you guys," their mother got involved. "Your father is very talented but he sits wasting away his talent. He's the one that makes us poor," she lamented.

"Mo-o-o-m," Faith dragged.

"He has a degree in Performing Arts," mom continued paying no attention to Faith. The mother sounded as if this was the first time she had revealed this to the children or like the children does not know that the father has a degree in that field. On many occasion, she had shared husband's 'hidden talent' and education in Theatrical Arts to acquaintances.

"Dad, can we go to the circus?" Maxwell asked as the father started the van engine and began to pull away.

Faith frowned at her brother, signifying the brother was going to cause the father to resume the vegetarian topic again.

"Another day," the father replied.

"How about today, it's the last day," Maxwell pointed out. As the father realized Sunday was the last day of the circus show, he consented.

"Okay guys," he said as he looked around to get everybody's approval.

"Okay!" Everyone agreed except Maxwell responded with a resounding "Yes!" demonstrating with his fist, half raised elbow with a downward thrust motion simultaneously with the 'YES'.

Meanwhile, Jeremiah at a glance noticed the sister crossing her fingers pointed towards the father.

"What are you doing?" he asked.

"I'm…I'm…." she chuckled intermittently as she explained to the brother. "I am trying to prevent dad talking about vegetarians and animal advocates again," everyone busted out laughing. Even the father couldn't help laughing too.

Crossing of the fingers is a presumptive sign to hopefully prevent any unwanted occurrence. An example presumption is a wish that it does not rain in a particular or eventful day. It's a common myth in some parts of Africa or the world at large. In this instance, Faith hoped the father does not resume the dominant topic. Funny! Huh!

"Good try daughter, good try," the father abruptly took over. "Your spell only works in Africa, see, we are in America over 5000 miles or 8000 km across many waters give and take which country in Africa is your mileage point. Most spells do not work when they are taken across oceans," the laughter that was still looming on everyone's face continued.

Their father turned into the Race Course where the circus is staged. At the entrance of the Race Course, they were greeted by angry group of protesters carrying signs with various phrases: 'ANIMALS, YOU ANIMALS!' referring to circus staff and supporters; 'DON'T GO, DON'T PATRONIZE, DON'T BE LIKE THEM'; 'RUN ELEPHANTS, RUN PUPPIES, RUN TIGERS, DON'T LET THEM ABUSE YOU, RUN, RUN'; 'I WISH YOU ALL BARBARIANS BURN IN HELL'.

"Can you believe this," their mother said in disbelieve as she read the signs.

The protesters literally treated the area like a war-zone shooting out chants, brandishing pickets in the air, marching around and creating trench-like marks on the grass with their shoes in a vicious cycle format.

"Get off the grass," their father with a snappy voice said to one of the protesters. "You are abusing and killing them too." The man looked silly and stupefied. "Yes, the grass, you are walking on are being abused by your feet/shoes," he firmly concluded with stern looks.

"That's not nice, Honey," the wife rebuked the husband. "Apologize to the man."

"I refused to do such thing," he replied. "Let him learn the hard way. Are you in support of their ignorance and foolishness," he looked at the wife.

"Let me be their teacher. Some people need *enlightenment*. I don't want to flow with the assumption that all animal advocates know what they are doing. Many are coated to be followers without clear knowledge of their actions," he pulled up to the man at the gate and paid $4.00 for parking.

As the family waited in line to purchased tickets a man tapped him on the shoulder. Ami turned to see who it was. The man appeared familiar to him.

"I'm sorry," Ami apologized. "Your face looked familiar but don't remember…."

"At the entrance few minutes ago when you drove in," the man explained before Ami could finish his lines. Ami's immediate recollection of a closed and one on one contact with any person at the entrance was the man that was collecting parking fees. Then he noticed a picket in the man's hand.

"I'm sorry if I offended you by what I said," Mr. Ami quickly apologized to about 6 feet tall white man. He wore prescribed glasses, long sleeved T-Shirt and faded jeans pants.

Mrs. Ami seemed afraid the man was going to pick a fight with the husband. She stared at the husband as if to say: 'I told you!'

"Ps.s.s.t," the boys, Jeremiah and Maxwell signaled each other to be ready should the man made any physical move at their father.

"My name is Lucas," he stretched his hand for a handshake.

"Mr. Lucas, nice to meet you, you can call me Inyang but I prefer, Ami," as both shook hands.

"You may leave the 'Mr.' out, just Lucas will suffice," he shared.

"Please forgive me if I attached 'Mr.' to your name again. I'm so much fond of it, it's a form of showing respect," Mr. Ami explained.

"It's understood," Mr. Lucas replied in agreement.

"Faith!" the mother called her attention. Faith was few feet away talking with a school mate she just met. She was unaware of what was happening.

"I'll be right there," she replied. "Mom, this is my friend, Gloria at school." Gloria waved at Faith's mother. Both girls resumed their conversation.

"I gotta go," Faith said to Gloria as she saw the mother walking towards them. Faith and the mother met half way. From her body language, it was obvious her mother was briefing her of what's going on with the father as they headed towards the line where the boys and father waited for their turn to purchase tickets. The man was still walking along and talking to Mr. Ami as he advanced towards the ticket window. Their conversation seemed normal rather than a conflict or heated argument.

"Dad is everything alright?" Faith asked the father.

"Yes! Yes!" he replied. "Please meet Mr. no Lucas. We are talking about vegetarians and animal-rights," he introduced and smiled about the use of 'Mr.' not too long since on that title issue.

"Hello! Sir," Faith greeted Mr. Lucas.

"Please call me, Lucas," he corrected as he shook Faith's hand with a grin on his face.

"O-okay," Faith responded with a smile. "Is my father bombarding you with vegetarian stuff," she asked along with a giggle.

"Absolutely," Lucas replied. "He sure got me to leave the protesting group to his side of the reasoning."

"Truth, not just reasoning," Ami cut in. "Truth based on facts. Animals, plants and vegetables alike may die if abused or killed."

"Look at this" (he twisted his right foot firmly pressing the sole of his shoe on the spot where he stood) he then bend down and picked up squelch grass and shown the damage done.

"You've made your point, I like that demonstration," Mr. Lucas commented.

"I'm Sold!" he exclaimed hurriedly because he did not want any interruption before he finished his thoughts.

Faith burst out laughing. Her father is semi-serious. Her mother and brothers became curious as to what was going on. Mr. Lucas joined Faith laughing. He was about to shook hands with Mr. Ami when a voice solicited to render service.

"May I help you sir," a female attendant asked through a small trailer window. "How many tickets please," she added.

"Six, if Lucas would join us," he looked at him as he reached for money to pay for the tickets. Lucas hesitated.

"It's my treat," Ami insisted.

"Okay! Okay! Since you insist," Lucas conceded. "I've come this far…"

"By faith," Ami jokingly added without giving Lucas a chance to finish his sentence. Everybody including Mrs. Ami, the boys, Jeremiah and Maxwell laughed uncontrollably.

"That will be $75.00," the attendant interrupted with a smile.

"Forgive us," Mr. Ami said to her as he handed the money to her.

"Thank you, enjoy the show!" She concluded as she handed the tickets to Mr. Ami.

"Mr. Lucas," Jeremiah called his attention. "We were ready for you thinking you were going to hit our dad with that picket in your hand." Dieudonnèe, Jeremiah's mom motioned him to stop but was already too late.

"Oh! No!" Mr. Lucas quickly replied and overlooked Jeremiah addressing him as Mr. Lucas. "I'm not like that," he suddenly realized he still had the picket in his hand. He discarded it immediately saying, "I don't need this anymore," as he stared at Mr. Ami. "I've learned so much from your father just under 30 minutes than in many years of ignorance or lack of *enlightenment*. Your dad has earned my respect."

Jeremiah patted him on the shoulder as they handed over the tickets to the usher at the tent arena entrance. Everyone got inside looking for seats. Maxwell, Jeremiah and their sister, Faith sat together not too far from their parents. Mr. Lucas sat with Mr. Ami and his wife, Dieudonnèe. Some children were already enjoying the Pony rides taking turns around the circus ring. Parents and guardians made a single-file formation along the rails separating the ring as they waited to get their little ones as they done riding the Pony. The arena was packed as spectators were still being ushered to their seats. The merchants were busy catering concessions going up and down the aisles.

"L…let the SHOW begins!" A baritone voice of the circus announcer bellowed short moment after they sat down.

"Are you rea…d…y!" he continued with a gesture directing attention towards different sitting areas of the tent arena.

"Yeah!" the crowd acknowledged with exploded response with a much-needed jolt of enthusiasm and electricity that filled the air. Many people in the crowd including children in reflective cone hats, necklace, eye glasses, magic wands, were waving all kinds of animal balloons, lit up swords and daggers and other assorted lights purchased at the concession stands or within the tent.

"Are you rea...d...y!" the announcer bellowed again, at least three consecutive times. The crowd got louder and wilder each time with chanting cheers and roars that circulated throughout every nooks and corners of the arena.

"Wow!" Lucas exclaimed. "I don't remember the last time I was at the circus. I'm going to kill my wife for this."

"Oh! No!" Ami cut in. "No more killings, there are too many dead grass around here already," he joked as he chuckled.

"I don't mean like that," Lucas said in defend with a guilty look. "I wouldn't be carrying signs here if it wasn't for her pressure."

"Don't blame your wife," Ami corrected. "You had a choice, yet you also made that choice. She didn't force you into it. You agreed with her reasoning back then on what you thought was justifiable. Do not even blame yourself. If you had heard another school of thought on the subject matter, likely would have placed you in a better position to respond differently. My..." as Mr. Ami was about to continue his philosophical briefings, the crowd interrupted with electrified cheers as the clowns, animals and other performers of all ranks made grand entrance.

"That's awesome!" Lucas exclaimed. "I wish my wife would leave that gate and..." interestingly his phone rang in the middle of his conversation.

"My wife," he announced to Ami.

"Aren't you going to answer?" Mr. Ami asked as Lucas put the phone back in his shirt pocket. "Wait, you meant to tell us you left your wife at the gate to confront me. That not enough, you are sitting here without her to see the circus."

"Loving," Ami called his wife's attention. "Guess what, Lucas' wife is outside by the main gate, in demonstration with the Animal Advocate groups."

"You mean it!" Mrs. Ami said in response without making a big deal to it.

"Alright, alright," Lucas signaled. "Let me explained. You don't know my wife. She won't come in even if invited. She is one of the 'ring leaders', I mean coordinators pushing for this course."

"You don't know that. She has not yet been challenged or *enlightened*. You weren't until today or should I say until now," Ami disputed.

"As I was about to say earlier but cut off by the crowd's alarming cheers, my aim is to share my view point and educate as many people as possible on this ignorance and negative perceptions. Wait, do not draw final conclusion yet till I may have met with your wife," Ami reminded and cautioned Lucas.

"Okay!" Lucas consented.

The circus took its full turn. The momentum changed gears. The announcer asked everyone to stand and joined in singing the National Anthem. Suddenly after the Anthem, the lights were out. The announcer's voice prompted the crowd to flick on their flashlights. Lights with different colors dominated the arena with screams of excitement from the crowd. Then the spotlights were on the center ring leaving the sitting areas dark with silhouette and spotted flashlights. The clowns, "Oh boy" keeps us laughing non-stop. The all-females acrobat took the ring, performed with suspended drapes up in the air. After this, the dogs were ushered in by two trainers. Each dog took turns jumping over different levels of vault. Each successful jump was applauded by the crowd.

"Check that out, amazing!" A voice behind Lucas echoed. "I can't wait for the tigers to show up," the voice sounded with anticipated excitement. Lucas turned to look who was talking but not someone known. However, he decided to engage the person with some remarks…

"I admired your excitement. You must have seen this before," Lucas asked.

"Yeah men, I don't miss any circus in town," the man behind Lucas responded. "I bring my children, Matt and Nancy since they were little," he shuffled their hair with his hand to identify for Lucas to know who his children were. "They loved it just as I do. How these animals response and performed as if they were humans is incredible. Some people can't even throw and catch a ball…" he was interrupted by another round of cheers from the crowd as he was about to continue.

The tigers were just led in by female and male trainers. These beautiful creatures walked in so gracefully without any indication they could hurt a fly. Conversely, these are the same creatures if left in their natural habitat are very dangerous, preyed and hunted other animals for food including human beings if they venture in their environment. Now they were so tamed and trained to obey the command of the trainers to entertain the spectators, amazing!

"Men, look!" The man signaled to Lucas. Both men stopped their conversation to watch the tigers performed. They kept the crowd going non-stop with cheering, performance after performance which included jumping, rolling, going through a ring of fire and taking a bow with their paws up in salute.

"What did I tell you, men," the man tapped Lucas on the shoulder again.

"The man got a point," Ami got involved and turned briefly to look at the man.

"He does," Lucas concurred. "Thank you sir, for the inspiration," Lucas gesture to the man. The man nodded but no words.

One man acrobatic performance followed by another clown appearance brought the show to intermission.

Lucas and I along with the boys decided to step outside for fresh air as it was so humid inside the tent. Faith and the mother remained.

Outside, we were greeted by Lucas' wife, Magdalene.

"Evening," Magdalene said abruptly as she dashed towards the husband. She cared less for any response to her salutation.

Maxwell and Jeremiah were about to exchanged greetings with her as she walked pass between them to the husband.

It did not take them long to figure Magdalene was in no mode to entertain additional greetings.

"What in the world were you doing inside and refused to take my call," she winked indicating to the husband, it was time to go. "Don't tell me you actually were watching the circus…" she acted hysterical, pacing back and forth.

"Mag…Mag, listen to me," Lucas tried to calm and get wife's attention…

"Let go of me!" his wife snapped. "I can't believe you ignored our course. We came to tell these ruthless people how animals are abused. We came to expose their mercilessness. We came (she increased the momentum after each phrase and brief pause) to tell them not to promote this despicable show. We came to tell them (referring to circus troupe) to stop punishing and ill-treating the animals…" her voice was pitched loud and clear that caught the attention of the people around us to stare.

Mr. Ami got in between their exchanges before Lucas' wife made another statement.

"Ma-am," Ami addressed her.

"Do I know you," she responded sharply as she blatantly stared at him.

"Do you have anything to do with this?" she asked and all worked up.

"Humbly yes," Ami bowed with a hand gesture showing respect. "My name is Inyang. It sounds like Chinese but it's Nigerian, nickname is Ami," he introduced himself with a sly smile.

"What does your name means? I know all your names have meanings," she sounded sort of judgmental.

"Deep and large body of waters - river or ocean," Ami shared with a smile.

"May I call you 'Rivers' if I forgot or can't pronounce 'E-e...' everyone forced to laughing.

"Inyang, it starts with 'I'," Mr. Ami clarified. 'I-N-Y-A-N-G,' he spelled. The laughing ensued further.

This was a real ice breaker especially on Magdalene's stand point. She was completely relaxed. She did not seem the same woman who, few moments ago was very angry. Mr. Lucas looked so relief as if a heavy load has just been lifted off his shoulders. The conversation took a 90o spin.

"That's a beautiful name," Magdalene complimented. The husband looked stun moving his eyes from his wife then on Ami and back to wife.

"Thank you," Ami acknowledged.

"My name is Magdalene but you can call me Margaret."

"It's well noted Margaret," Ami assured.

"You didn't tell me the meaning of your name," Lucas pointed accusing finger at Ami.

"You did not ask," Ami fired back with friendly gesture. "Now you know, thanks to your wife," Ami fixed his eyes on Magdalene.

"Jokes aside, we don't have much time before the circus resumed," Ami looked at both husband and wife. A brief silence ensued. A little tension is felt by the parties.

"Count me out," Magdalene objected. "Lou," she called and looked at her husband, Lucas, "We are going home, aren't we?"

"Not so fast," Ami quickly acted. Lucas in suspicious anticipation of resistance by his wife hid his face pretended to look at Maxwell and Jeremiah but without saying anything to them.

"Margaret, you have free admission. Tickets sales are closed. Before you objected again, please come inside and show me how and if the animals are really abused. Do not act on hearsay. See for yourself. To see is believable as generally maintained," Ami appealed. Magdalene reluctantly consented but without some caution.

"I feel so foolish doing this," she said as she took a deep breath. "I'm betrayed! I betray them! I've let them down!" she exclaimed. "I hope they (referring to SOFAR) don't catch me doing this," she exacerbated the scenario pacing back and forth.

"No you've not betrayed anyone," Ami said with empathy. "You are on the path of knowledge and discoveries. I hope your group listened to you as you took back what you are about to discover. I hoped you are not a vegan," he abruptly added and totally changed the path of the conversation.

"Why?" Magdalene asked with suspicious and innocence looks.

"Veganism, that's an extreme of vegetarianism!" Ami exclaimed. "Vegans totally altered vegetarian theory. They do not consume any animal food or dairy products including cosmetic products that were tested on animals. Worst still the orthodox vegans boycott stores that sell these products. They do not use any products derived from animals."

"Do you mean products like shoes, clothes …fur, silk, leather," Magdalene elaborated the lists.

"Hats, earrings, etc..." Ami picked up naming other items before Magdalene could come up with another thing on her mind.

"Earrings," Magdalene pondered. "What part of animal could an earring be possibly made?" she questioned, her husband also eagerly waiting to hear an answer.

"The animal teeth, paws, bones…" Ami numerated.

"Oh Jesus," Magdalene reacted partly amused.

"Thanks Heavens for the provisions!" Lucas exclaimed. It seemed like he was about to say more but the wife quickly resumed so she would not lose trend of thoughts.

"I'm gonna tell it, I'm gonna tell them," she picked up energy in her expressions.

"You mean your, no our group?" her husband asked sarcastically.

"Yes! Yes!" Magdalene responded with full body gesture but paused and bluffed when she discovered it was her husband who asked the question. "I bet some of us would have difficulty distinguishing which of the earrings won is made with animal stuff," she released a sigh of relief and somewhat disenchanted.

"However, Mr. Ami regained where he left off at. They (vegans) do not see or should I say, do not realize anything wrong consuming plants and plants products. What's wrong with that theory?" He paused. "Brenda Brooks Miles in her book, <u>*We Eat to Live not Live to Eat with*</u> <u>*Key to Health*</u> said, 'I admit that for quite a period of time spent on vegetarian books I developed and detested meat, however I am in the satisfactory level described by Roland Rogers in his memoir', 'It appears that he had been convinced to embraced vegetarianism and had resolved that he would not dared touched to consume the meat from animals for the simple fact behind how ruthlessly animals are slaughtered, when indeed they rightfully do not deserved such ordeal. But looking at the other side of the coin he was extremely fond of consuming fish….'"

"Pescatarian…" Magdalene began to identify the type of vegetarian Roland Rogers was but Ami's voice amplified hers.

"Pescatarian, Pescetarian, I believed means the same thing," he paused for confirmation.

"Yes they mean the same thing," Magdalene concurred. "These groups do not eat meat and animal flesh but do eat fish," she clarified.

"Well, to Miles and Rogers," Ami continued. "The fish and the vegetables that you are so fond of eating are also ruthlessly slaughtered, cooked, fried or shushed. In all fairness, they do not deserve that ordeal either regardless who is consuming them."

"You made a point there," Magdalene observed. "Who is Brenda Brooks Miles?" she asked.

"Brenda Miles was the Former Chairman of Public Health Concern Committee of Women's Association, Upper District, USA," Ami answered.

"Now you've seen the controversy this has created. What are much amusing are the other groups of vegans. Raw-Vegan does not eat any animal by-products or anything cooked well-done that may kill all enzymes and nutrients. Processed food items like breads, sugars…are out of their liking. Their theories are: no killing, no processing no cooking. Wow! No killing? Are you kidding me? Get this, you kill the plants raw, you bit them raw, you chew them raw…"

Magdalene and her husband, the only two at this point into the conversation, laughed at Ami's last gig puzzle remarks.

"You think that is funny. What do you make of the Plant based Vegans who avoid greasy or refined, starchy food items such as chips, fries, white rice, white bread, white sugar (I branded these the 'whites family')" Another round of laughter from the trio followed.

"Wait, wait," Ami hurriedly cut the laughter but to add: Junk Food Vegans who care less about healthy living. They go for white bread, chips, fries, Oreos, twizzler candies, faux meat…"

"The lists continue," Lucas cut in abruptly with a vaguely giggle that others did not participate.

"Margaret," Ami summoned. "On a personal note, have you ever roasted, cooked vegetables? Have you ever burned logs in the fire place to warm your home? Yet you advocate for animals being abused. Please follow the description how the logs ignite after few minutes in contact with fire. The flame saunters slowly along the stems before gaining momentum with sparks and crackling sounds (literally crying unnoticed.) Hmm dead logs you may acclaim. The dead logs were once full of lives but mercilessly chopped down by the hands of human beings to serve their heinous purposes. Logs once full of lives with enough of nutrients and liquid to sustain them yet hewed down senselessly by man and ended up in the heath at your house. That charred logs turned to ashes and charcoal. Christmas Trees are cut down every Fall Season, near electrocution with electric wires tangled all over them every year during Christmas time to decorate your homes. Trees are uprooted to provide vacant lots to build our houses. Here and there each year, News of deforestation is featured in a given region. That warning crackling sounds symbolized the tree's everlasting defenseless and unfruitful liberation movement and protest since its inception," he paused for few seconds.

"If I may continue, have you ever used spinach or cut lettuce for salad? If you do not prepare them by yourself, at least you have eaten them in the restaurants or elsewhere. However, have you for once paused, or have you had a second thought that everything we eat – raw or processed were all Living Things and once had life? Wouldn't you agree from your prospective notion of looking at life in particular and things in general that plants too deserve to live just like other Living Things if you still press for the rights of animals. I hope I'm not boring you with my theoretical truth," Ami paused to ask.

"No!" both Lucas and Magdalene said at the same time. Magdalene looked at the husband as if to say: this is my turn to hear this.

"If you don't eat meat…" Ami resumed but got interrupted.

"I do eat meat, only Mag is a vegetarian," Lucas selfishly ignored the wife's unclear warning and but be on the defensive side. The wife winked her eyes in his direction the second time.

"As I was saying," Ami picked up where he left off. "If you don't eat meat yet eat vegetables, you are as guilty as those who eat meat. The truth is, you are as heartless to the vegetables, plants and trees alike. If you condemn meat eaters (the animal group in the animal kingdom) called carnivores or omnivores those that eat both animals and plants. You should condemn yourselves the herbivores (plants-only-eaters) and check your conscience for consuming vegetables as substitute to meat. If you point one accusing finger at meat consumers, realized the rest of your fingers are equally directing at you for consuming and destroying vegetable lives," he took his time in narrative style to this point.

Magdalene and Lucas attention on Ami as he lectured them became undisturbed. Nothing at this point could distract them. One could tell they were so much into it.

"You are inhumane to vegetables and plants," he dropped the phrase like a bomb. Lucas shyly nodded in agreement. One can sense the amount of pressure that loomed around his body language.

"Among our group we also have Flexitarian – the semi vegetarians," Lucas breathe a sigh of relief as he proudly announced, I'm in this group. We mostly eat vegetarian diet but occasionally eat meat. Others are the Lacto-ovo who don't eat beef, pork, poultry, fish, shellfish or animal flesh of any kind but do eat eggs and dairy products."

"This is delightful! I never knew about these many kinds of vegetarians," Maxwell broke attention from his brother to listen to Lucas.

"I'm not done," Lucas was so pomp. "If you split up Lacto-ovo, you will have Lacto Vegetarians who do not eat eggs but eat dairy products. Then Ovo Vegetarians are reverse of the former. They do not consume dairy products but do eat eggs."

"But why is it so?" Maxwell was now curious and very much into the explanation Lucas was about to provide.

"It is because they are lactose intolerant," Lucas explained.

"Okay! It made sense," Maxwell appeared satisfied.

"The last group is Macrobiotic Vegetarians: they eat unprocessed vegan foods like whole grains, fruits, vegetables, here and there do eat fish but they don't eat sugar, refined oils are out of the equation," Lucas finished at last.

This seemed to have given consolation to Lucas from what appeared obvious he had been under pressure and several attacks by the hands of his wife and some of her friends for refusing to stop eating meat. It also appeared like a heavy load just got lifted off him again after these expressions possibly held in for a very long time. But here at that moment he was not under any kind of fire, not vulnerable to any opposition.

"Are you not tired of stepping on the grass and plants on your bid to speak for the animals?" Ami drew Magdalene's attention again to reality. "Can't you feel their struggles to be released from under your feet?" He paused and became intense with painting the mind alluding pictures.

"Again I repeat, you advocate for the animals the way they are killed or how they are eaten or how they are abused but you do not advocate for the vegetables and plants that suffer the same way. That's dire selfishness on your own part. You kill and consume plants to sustain your lives. These plants that give you the energy to picket in defend of animals. Why? Think! Think again. Think hard. Learn to separate feelings over reason," the bomb Ami now just dropped exploded with much impact.

"Please stop, Mr. Ami," Magdalene begged. The few minutes with Ami and his ideology seemed like hours and tended to weigh her down mentally.

"You make me; no, make us (SOFAR) feel like monsters," she lamented. She scanned her eyes like searching for some sort of support. She looked overwhelmed listening to accusations but at the same time tried to make some senses out of the whole theories.

"Now you see how meat consumers and circus staff feel when you labeled them as barbarians," Ami reminded her by reflecting on some of the signs Magdalene's group carried and displaced.

"You've never thought about that like this until now. Let me try and see if I can succeed getting some of them to see the light and participate in this new campaign: *Eat Live and Let's Live*," Ami switched to sympathize.

"Should we go in now, the show is about to begin," Ami looked simultaneously at both Lucas and Magdalene.

"Let's go! Why not," Magdalene said along with a hand signal. Her husband looked so surprise but without a word. However, his facial expression was more than words, likely saying within himself, is this the same woman a moment ago that almost 'buried me alive' for going in to see the circus show with Ami's family.

"Mr. Inyang," a female voice rang from behind. Ami turned to see who called.

"Well, well, well, Ms. Bradshaw," Ami responded.

"Abigail," he called as he squad to the same height and eye level of a little girl with Bradshaw.

"Huh," the girl replied.

"Lucas, Margaret, meet Ms. Bradshaw and her granddaughter, Abigail," Ami made the introductions. "We work together," he added.

"Call me Beatrice," Ms. Bradshaw seemed to correct but quickly added, "The Agency we work for has sold our first names out for the sake of professionalism. So we addressed one another including other co-workers by their last names. However, it's nice to meet both of you."

"It's a pleasure meeting you and your granddaughter too," Lucas responded as he extended his hand to shake Beatrice and Abigail.

"Likewise," Magdalene exchanged handshakes with Beatrice. "I see you brought your granddaughter to the circus," she added.

"She is so pretty," Magdalene complimented.

"Thank you!" Abigail's tiny sweet voice echoed as she swung her body side to side modeling her beauty to the compliment. Smiles beamed on every face in reaction to the little girl pose.

"I always bring her every time any circus came to this area," Beatrice acknowledged.

Mr. Lucas appeared uneasy and wore a guilty face as if to confess to some secret. Of course, this was the second time tonight he had been directly reminded about children being brought to the circus. As he was about to speak, the wife came with a question.

"So Mr. Rivers, what is then your first name?" Magdalene asked, purposely chose and had fun with 'Rivers'. Everyone forced to smile even before he could answer as they brought into remembrance the fun associated earlier when Magdalene struggled to get the pronunciation of the last name right during the name drill.

"Akpan," A-K-P-A-N, he spelled just as he did his last name earlier to be sure the party involved knows how the alphabets are arranged or correctly knows how name is written.

"What does it mean? If I remembered correctly, your last name, 'Inyang' means 'River' Magdalene asked and expounded. The smiles that were still on faces lingered on.

"You are great with your memory," Ami complimented Magdalene along with a soft hand clap. "My first name is a title or acronym to designate the first born male of any family," he began. "For example, if I was to designate your first son from your second son, I would say: 'Akpan Margaret or Akpan Lucas.' Anyone hearing that immediately would know which of your sons was born first, and your second son would be 'Udo', U-D-O, he concluded.

"That's interesting," Lucas excitedly proclaimed.

Beatrice nodded in confirmation. She had been through this process before with Ami.

"Lou, so you are 'Akpan,' Magdalene pointed out her husband's birth rite.

"Do you have a title for me?" she quickly added. "I am the first daughter," she paused as if she has more to add but flinched.

"You are Adiaha, me too," Beatrice jumped to provide an answer but stumbled on the pronunciation.

"That's amazing, you surprised me," Ami exalted Beatrice on her memory. Names tales and their meanings had common place at work environment.

"That's astounding," Magdalene expressed as she fixed her eyes on Beatrice. Beatrice face beamed with smiles.

"A-D-I-A-H-A," Ami spelled and correctly pronounced. "All these titles could be used as names if so desired. That was my mother's name," he concluded.

"Here we go again with spelling," Beatrice jokingly made the remarks as Ami finished the name spelling.

"Pop," Jeremiah called the father. He tapped on his wrist though he did not wear a wrist Watch indicating it was time to go in as he and Maxwell stepped next to the father. The father forced a smile in response to Jeremiah's gesture as he introduced them.

"Meet my boys, Jeremiah and Maxwell," Ami directed Beatrice's and Magdalene's attention to his children.

"Hello guys," Beatrice greeted them. "I met your sister, Faith but not you." Both of them responded in return to the salutation.

"It's a pleasure meeting you both," Magdalene extended her hand and took turns shaking hands with them. Jeremiah and Maxwell couldn't conceal their facial expressions going back to previous encounter with her when they attempted to greet her. She looked at the husband for his queue to greet the boys.

"Mag, I already met them," Lucas enlightened the wife.

"Okay! Let's go in," Ami led in the front. They all filed behind him going back in for the show. Inside, many children were in line chaperoned by parents and guardians to ride on the elephants. This exercise kept the children and guardians busy during the intermission.

Beatrice parted with the group, took granddaughter by hand and cued behind the last person in line for the elephant ride.

While the ride was taking place the circus crew was setting up for second round of the show. The atmosphere was captivating with spectators moving around the arena either going back to their seats, calling vendors for snacks and drinks or just hanging around for the shows to commence.

"Margret, this is my wife, Dieudonnée and my daughter, Faith," Ami made the introduction as he made room for Magdalene to sit. "She preferred to be addressed as Margaret instead of Magdalene," he alerted.

"How are you, Margaret?" Dieudonnée asked Magdalene as both of them exchanged handshakes.

"I'm fine, thanks for asking," Magdalene responded. "Pleasure meeting you," she rested.

"You can call me Dieu. Faith, shake her hand," Dieudonnée directed her daughter. She stepped aside to make room so her daughter could shake hands with Magdalene. Magdalene and Faith shook hands parting with smiles. Dieudonnée then looked at Lucas as in approval to allow his wife sit next to her.

"What name did you say I can call you? I bet it must have some meaning to it," Magdalene inquired with anticipation.

"Dieu, D-I-E-U," she spelled. Magdalene chuckled in reference to spelling of the name just as Dieudonnée's husband did. This now became an indicator of their norms whenever their names are asked or shared. They just want to make sure people get their names correctly.

"Dieu" is short form of Dieudonnée which means 'God-given' or 'Gift of God'. Dieu means 'God'. She is generally addressed as such by friends and peers. That 'god' at times assumed conservative nature depending who is using it. However, she could be tuff with it like she is "God" in some instances.

"I love it! Dieu," Magdalene exclaimed.

Suddenly the lights went out leaving the arena glittering with flashlights. The announcer's voice followed. When the lights came back on, only the performing ring was lit. Clowns were running everywhere. They featured at intervals throughout the rest of the show. A section of the ring was up with a globe-like structure for motor cycle rides. The riders were next to performed. They glided around the globe with seemingly dangerous moves as they picked up speed each round. Magdalene was spellbound but cheering in relief at the end. She exchanged words with Dieudonnée who was also rigid on the seat.

Next were the elephants (including a baby elephant) with trilling performances in spite of their sizes. They stood with all four legs on small stools. The female trainer got picked up with the trunk. They formed a ring by placing the forelegs on the back of the one in front as they processed around the circle. They made the same formation using the trunks held to another's tail. They rounded up with a semi upright stand to salute the spectators with their forelegs. Every round of their profound performances equally received explosive ovation.

"Awesome!" Lucas exclaimed.

"What's awesome about using whip on them to perform," Magdalene countered the husband's enthusiastic expression.

"That whip would not hurt a fly," Ami exaggerated in response as Lucas looked at him speechless in reaction to wife's remarks.

"You missed something," Ami leaned closer to Magdalene as he explained further. The elephants were dismissed and led away by the trainer still fluttering the whip as they exit.

"Watch the whip, follow the whip closely," he redirected Magdalene's attention and focus. Lucas also adjusted his demeanor to focus as well.

"I am," Magdalene observed as prompted. "The whips are not on the animals," she consciously shared.

"Thank you, that's great!" Ami could not hide his excitement with the outcome.

"The whips are flung in the air to produced sounds to cue the animals and direct them. You are right. It's all in my head. The abuse theory has lodged in my head too long. Over the years I have nurtured the concept of how these animals are trained. Of course a much different pictures are being painted with the abuse theory," Magdalene concluded descriptions to her observation. Lucas briefly stood up (but quickly sat down so not to blocked others views) in reaction to wife's conscientious agreement to that piece of information. A quick looked at him revealed he was holding back oral and vocal expressions to the obvious results.

"Well, to see is to believe! It's said," Ami proclaimed. "I'm glad you've seen it now for yourself. I bet, if the whips were used on the animals repeatedly, those animals will bulldozed the trainers and make them history – of course I am not ruling out the true stories of abused animals. There are also true stories of abused and hungry animals preying on their abusers," all who listened to Ami nodded.

Another gripping performance was walking, dancing and somersaulting on a rope tied to two poles in the air. The audience was in for a treat. The evening closed with a thunderous canon shot vaulted out a performer into a hung net. The crowd went wild as usual with a fervent electric atmosphere.

When we stepped outside some minutes after 5:00 PM, the sun was still glimmering though inside the tent arena the mental inclination felt like it was late at night. Lucas and Magdalene spent a brief moment with the Ami's family as each took turn to say bye.

"This has been a memorable meeting and evening," Mr. Lucas excitedly shared.

"My husband is right," Magdalene agreed. "Mr. Rivers," she purposely took delight in using 'Rivers' again, paused to make sure she had his attention. "I apologized for being high strong headed the way I did," she winked.

"Oh please, it was all meant for good," Ami politely brushed-off.

"You should write a book so many people could be reached with this brilliant idea," Magdalene encouraged.

"Go Dad!" Faith acclaimed. "Now you've got your confirmation about writing." "Thanks Margaret," Faith concluded and waved.

Magdalene waved as her and her husband started walking away.

"Sure will do," Ami gladly accepted. "I'll make sure both of you are featured in my book."

"Bye!" everyone echoed.

The family got in the van and pulled off heading home. Along the way they came across team of soccer players playing soccer in a field. The sight of this game sparked reaction in Mr. Ami. But nothing unfamiliar because he used to be a soccer player himself while in his birth country.

"Grass, Grass! Grass! If they are not killed on a circus arena, then it is at a soccer or football field. Look at them (referring to the players) dribbling and tackling each other; running carelessly all over the grass mindless what's beneath their feet. They completely yank them up down to the roots with their boots. Yet no one speaks for them. No one pickets. No chants, no marching, no…"

"No advocates," Maxwell jokingly added, completing the thought progression for the father but seriously and well received by his father. He then searched for further details he could safely share to stay on in the discussion. Finding none, he changed the topic.

He brought up a seemingly conversation that transpired between a child and a father. Maxwell had heard this from a comedian. He attempted to deliver a replica of same but his accent was way off the original work.

"Papa what's for breakfast," the son asked.

"Son, yam and beans," the father replied.

"Papa what's for lunch," the son asked.

"Son, yam and beans," the father replied.

"Papa what's for dinner," the son asked.

"Son, yam and beans," the father replied.

Maxwell busted out laughing after he finished the joke. He laughed not because of the phrases involved but how it was said and sounded in deep, thick and heavy Nigerian accent mimicked by the comedian. Others also erupted into laughter. Maxwell laughed for the most part, hysterically loud and extensive. He continued to laugh with full energy involving literally every muscle of the face, head, hands expressions, rocking body back and forth and stamping feet as he laughed. Jeremiah, Faith, the parents were trying hard to stopped laughing but were forced to laugh along with him as he adversely put on a semi show to the family.

Maxwell had got into trouble several times in school due to his funny way of laughing. He would continue to laugh when everyone has stopped, even when the subject matter or object of laughter no longer funny or not welcomed. His laughter has no boundaries. It engulf from hilarious subjects to sad to very emotional topics. The father recalled an incident at school that warranted him to be invited to a conference by the Vice Principal concerning Maxwell's behavior after the teacher had ordered every student to stop laughing in class.

The Vice Principal told a story of how the trouble started. A student's (Maxwell's classmate) home was caught on fire. The student had shared with the class how he lost a hamster in the fire.

"What a pity! What an innocent hamster caught in flames of living hell, similar to vegetables' fate in the oven, pot or hot pan," Ami paused to add to his reflection.

However, the manner the student presented the story invoked generic laughter in the classroom among the students including the teacher. The laughter escalated when the teacher appealed to the students to share said incident with their parents and families when they got home to solicit for donations to assist the victim's (student) family.

Instantly, one compassionate student stood up and announced he had $1.00 (obviously his snacks money) to donate. Everyone couldn't afford but to laugh. However, Maxwell's outburst was overwhelming. When all were ordered by the teacher to stop, Maxwell continued becoming disruptive as the teacher resumed teaching. Boom! That's how Maxwell got himself in trouble with the school authority.

"Papa what's for dinner," Faith joined in enjoying every moment of the jokes.

"Son, yam and beans," Jeremiah and Maxwell responded in unison. This created another episode of laughter.

Yam and beans is a typical combined, well balanced nutritious African meal likely other continents of the world. The combo is rich in carbohydrate and protein nutrients. The dish is basically common and readily available to both the rich and the poor people especially the poor who may not have the means to provide different stylish dishes often. The comedian was making fun of the commonality of this meal suitable for three square meals: breakfast (yam and beans), lunch (yam and beans), and dinner (yam and beans.)

The father saw another window of opportunity in the jokes to capitalize on his reasoning with vegetarians/animal advocates obnoxious attitude toward meat consumers. He basically doesn't have anything against them except their ignorant condemnation of the later.

"Those yams and beans once had life," he began. "Those yams and beans once were Living Things before they ended up in human pots – dead. They once were alive before being gulped down by humans to fat their bellies," he ended. Everyone broke up laughing again.

"Do you wanna know something," he injected in the slang word. "I don't blame the so call vegetarians. Most of them are ignorant; some of them naïve; while some lacked the knowledge of factual Biblical Creation Story as found in the Book of Genesis. I don't blame them because majority of them are misled by others who do not or refused to know the truth themselves. I called a faction of them, hypocrites."

"Watch out!" he exclaimed and picked up momentum. "Majority of them will return to eat meat again when they know the truth. They will learn to co-exist with meat consumers. They will limit the blame game after they read my book. Their advocacy is a reckless human policy. The messages these demonstrations send to our children and the uneducated is troubling. The advocates should not be in a position of denying and justifying that killing animals for meals is barbaric and inhumane but killing plants for meals are permissible and humanly so."

"Honey," the wife called the husband's attention with the endearing name. "Please don't forget to stop at Walsh's Farm. I got to pick some stuff to prepare meal."

"Hello Mr. Walsh," Mr. Ami greeted as he entered the kiosk.

"Hello Rev," Walsh replied.

"Rev" as Walsh took delight in addressing Mr. Ami is an abbreviation of "Reverend." Rev was a Pastor of an area church where Walsh worshipped and fellowshipped with other Christians. He had been the pastor there for over

11 years. His dedication to the ministry impacted and transformed many lives including Mr. Walsh.

Faith took her turn after the father to greet Walsh.

"How are your brothers?" Walsh asked Faith.

"They are in the van," she answered.

"Where's my angel?" Walsh asked referring to Faith's mother who did not yet stepped out of the vehicle. "My angel" was Walsh reminiscent way of addressing Dieudonnée who played a miraculous role to have and keep him in church, saved his almost destroyed life from unprecedented divorce and death of his only son few years back. Just as he was about to continue conversation with Faith, he noticed Dieudonnée approaching.

"Oh there she comes!" He looked at her direction.

"My angel, I just asked about you," Walsh stepped forward to give her greetings.

"Sorry my dear, I was trying to get my boys to come out," Dieudonnée explained. "But they didn't see the need for everyone to come in shopping for few fruits, vegetables and other items," she quirked.

"That's boys!" He emotionally exclaimed with his departed son on mind. "It is the thoughts of men that are deceptive, their oaths that are obscure," he added with the unknown quote and origin. He severally had used this quote on any occasion he's reminded of his son, which he linked to the actions of his wife that resulted in their divorce.

"I sensed how difficult this is to you," Dieudonnée empathized. "However, this is a new chapter of your life which is going to open many pages of opportunities," she encouraged. "Look at this business you had abandoned and lost. It's fully operative and doing well. My brother, what you had lost, you shall regained by the hands of your Almighty God. He did it for Job He'll do it for you," she wished. (Job is a biblical character who lost all he had including children but was blessed twice as much as he had before)

"Amen!" Her husband echoed.

"Amen!" Everyone joined in chorus including the boys who have decided to come out from the van to join the family specifically to come and said hello to Mr. Walsh.

"Hi Mr. Walsh," Jeremiah and Maxwell simultaneously greeted.

"Hey guys!" Walsh reached out and shook their hands in turn respectively.

"Mr. Walsh you looked so good, you trimmed your beard, well groomed," Jeremiah complimented.

"I had to move on," Walsh responded but suddenly quiet. His melancholy mood was obvious.

"We apologized, we didn't intend to expose you to this feeling," Jeremiah tendered.

"No need to apologize. It's not your fault. At times I got carried away in emotion when instances triggered my memory," Walsh resolved. He padded both brothers on their shoulders.

Soon afterwards a Jeep pulled in the lot. Two teenage siblings, a boy and a girl got out and ran towards the Kiosk. There was an indicator they had been here before. The boy got to Walsh first and gave him a high-five clap. The girl followed with arms around Walsh's waist.

"You must be coming back from the circus," Walsh stated.

"How did you know," the girl asked.

"Your father exposed your little mission," Walsh revealed with a smile.

"Yes I did my butterfly," her father confirmed and kissed her on the forehead.

"Rev meet my neighbor Andrew, I called him Andy," Walsh called Ami's attention after a brief conversation with Andy as they stepped closer to Ami. His wife, Jewel is truly a gem.

"We met not long ago," Andrew asserted. "At the circus," he quickly added because he picked a stare and blank expression on Ami's face.

Ami still had no recollection of meeting him at the circus. He wondered could this be another member of SOFAR that must have spotted him at the arena. He only directly had closed contact and interactions with Lucas and Magdalene. Andrew realized Ami was still lost in memory he provided more detail.

"I sat on the next row behind you. I had few conversations with the man that sat next to you," Andrew reminded.

"Oh Lucas, now I remember," Ami admitted. "Wow! What a coincident and a small world. That was my first time to know the man, Lucas that sat next to me. I challenged him at the race course gate. He was one of the animal advocate demonstrators."

"You mean SOFAR," Andrew asked just to be at the same page with Ami.

"Yes SOFAR but I was successful to convinced him to see the circus with us even later his wife," Ami proudly maintained.

"How did you do that? I'm not so much in tuned with SOFAR. They picket just about every year. The crowd got larger each year don't seemed to be affected by their demonstrations. I enjoy circus, my kids loved it. That's why I take them every year," Andrew shared.

"I *enlightened* them about their fear that circus animals in particular are being abused and animals in general are killed for meat. Of course my stand and effort is to balance the perceptions that both animals and plants in general are victims, killed for meals regardless who consumed which," Ami shared.

"Brilliant!" Andrew supported. "Walsh mentioned you are his spiritual father and mentor. He spoke very highly about you and your wife in most of our conversations. He is a good man. I hope he would heal from the reality of losing his son. He is so attached to my son, Matt," Andrew set the tone of great friendship with his neighbor, Walsh.

"Yes Andy, pleasure meeting you," Ami shook hands with Andrew and directed his attention on an entirely different approach to show him what he meant by *enlightenment* on the subject.

Ami picked a tomato from the shopping basket in his left hand. He threw the tomato in the air and caught it as he consecutively called Walsh for his attention.

"Mr. Walsh," Ami called.

"Yes Rev," Walsh replied.

"Would you say, this is a Living Thing?" he showed the tomato as a Food for Thought.

Walsh looked confused and surprised to the question. He hesitated an answer trying for a moment to figure out why the question. He stepped up to take a closer look at the tomato in question. Could he had placed a bad tomato on the shelves unnoticed, he wondered. More so, he was cautious of any answer he provided is correct. Couple months ago he had provided unacceptable answers to a similar question –

"A farmer and a butcher, who is guilty of murder?" was the question Ami asked.

"The butcher," Walsh had answered. When he was asked why, he said: "the butcher slaughters the animals."

"Both," Ami had disagreed and corrected. According to his opinion, while it is true the butcher slaughter the animals, it is also true the farmer kill the plants at harvesting.

"Don't feel bad Walsh," he consoled him. "You are doing what you do for a good cause, for the sake of humanity – to save lives. The creator gave us permission to have dominion over them," Ami had rested his argument.

As Walsh was about to say something in response to Ami's question on the tomato, Dieudonnée called Walsh's attention.

"Mr. Walsh, don't mind my husband," she said as she inspected the ears of the corn. "Your Rev had engaged us on the fact that God gave man the privilege to use plants and animals for food."

"Not again!" Walsh said comically. "Your husband called me a murderer last time he was here." Everyone laughed.

"Why?" Faith and the mother asked simultaneously…

"Did he really call you a murderer?" Dieudonnée finished the question eagerly. Even Jeremiah and Maxwell including Andrew became curious for his explanation.

"He had asked me: 'the butcher and the farmer, who was guilty of murder?'" Walsh shared.

"Who did you say…?" Dieudonnée posed the question.

Out of heightened curiosities each except Ami who was grinning and enjoying the moment, hurriedly called for an answer from Walsh.

"What was your answer?" Faith asked.

"Well, may we know what your opinion was?" Jeremiah followed.

"Did you give a satisfactory answer to my Dad?" Maxwell doubted as reflective in his demeanor.

"I'm waiting good neighbor, what was your call on it," Andrew used a funny teasing tone.

"Hold on guys!" Walsh became hesitant and very serious suddenly especially now under heightened pressure. "I pointed at the butcher. I blamed the butcher because I thought: gee, he's the one that terminate and he's the one that take the lives of animals. But your father quickly drew my attention in another direction – at me, a farmer. Suddenly it dawned on me. I reminiscent how each day, every week yanking these plants from their roots. I trimmed them. I plucked them. I picked them. I cut them without a second thought, without any consciousness. Some of the plants I walked over them, I stepped on them and I wrecked them without any consideration whatsoever they are Living Things as are animals."

"The alarming knowledge, the turning point was the fact that, I did not notice any struggle or resistance from them. No screams from them, no 'blood' as per red liquid flowing from them. Of course, what did I know or what did I care," Walsh continued to narrate.

"Guys," Walsh called out very loud as if addressing a large audience. "I cooked them, you boiled them, we roasted them and we ate them. Mind you, these are not animals we so much would protect but plants also Living Things. Your father was right, Rev is right!"

"Well said Walsh," Ami supported Walsh's analysis. "Everyone meet with Andrew, he was at the circus with his lovely children," he introduced. His family acknowledged and waved. None of them said a word to Andrew or the children because all eyes were on Walsh. Ami then shocked everyone, demonstratively squeezed the tomato in his hand and indicated to Walsh to include damaged tomato in his bill.

"Watch out Dad," Jeremiah jumped back as the squirts from the tomato almost got him.

"Oops, sorry son," he apologized. "The veggie blood almost got you," he said as he giggled.

"That's not funny," his wife said shyly in disapproval of his sarcastic action.

"Daddy you are definitely going too far," Faith reacted in a respectful way as she walked outside towards the van. One could easily notice her effort to conceal the urge to burst out laughing.

"Go ahead daughter, let it out," her father caught her off guards revealing her vulnerability.

Faith picked up her partially dropped face. She covered her mouth with her hands. She quickly leaped into the van. Everyone by now could hear her laughing hysterically so loud.

"Bye Mr. Walsh, bye Mr. Andy," Maxwell greeted with a grin as he stepped out to join the sister in the van.

"Maxwell come back and help carry these things to the van," his mother instructed as she checked out the items.

"Mom I got it," Jeremiah volunteered.

"Loving, add this to the list of Living Things to be devoured," Ami alerted his wife with the endearing name as he walked toward the check-out counter with a bunch of bananas.

"They are my favorable culprits," he shared with Walsh and Andy as he placed the bananas by the Register. His wife nodded in agreement and disagreement to the word, 'culprit' instead of fruit.

"I kill them most of the times. I struck the final blow after its rough journey from the farms, bruised as they were loaded and off loaded the trucks and transported to different destinations like your warehouse and kiosk," he described with humor.

"Honey," Dieudonnée dearly addressed the husband. "Mr. Walsh got the message," she ended with a chuckle.

Mr. Walsh could not help but joined in the chuckle even Andy enjoyed the moment.

"That will be $25.55 but even 25 okay," Walsh tendered.

Dieudonnée turned looking at the husband for money. All parties smiled.

"Here we go Walsh," Ami handed him the money.

"Mr. Walsh so long, I cherished the moment. Sir, he referred to Andy because his name skipped his memory, nice to meet you too," Jeremiah bid farewell as he exited the Kiosk.

Ami and Dieudonnée both waved and said goodbye at the same time to Walsh, Andrew and his children. Walsh too along with Andrew and his children did the same.

"Dad, I didn't know you were this serious with the vegetarian stuff until now listening to Mr. Walsh's episode of you and him," Jeremiah confronted the father as they hit the road again heading home. "It was fascinating!" He exclaimed.

"Come to think about it, people do certain things without a second thought, like chopping and eating vegetables but not conscious enough that they are killing them just as animals are killed for food," Jeremiah continued with his observation.

"We need to launch an awareness campaign to *enlighten* the public especially the critics that are ignorantly bias how animals are treated, slaughtered and consumed. A common misconception must be looked at," Jeremiah resuscitated the conversation.

"Jeremiah is absolutely right!" Maxwell said in a stronger and deeper tone to emphatically expressed support of his brother's notion. "Some people are busy pointing accusing fingers at others but forgot the rest of the fingers are directed towards them. I am sick of people that consider themselves as 'saints' when actually they have questionable and hidden spots of their characters and lives. That's exactly what brainwashed vegetarians and animal advocates and the likes are to the truth," Maxwell paused with a sigh.

"Now that I'm looking from a new perspective," Maxwell quickly continued so that no one interrupted his trend of thought. "What does it really matter now to any group(s) if an animal or chicken or seafood were tranquilized, shot with gun or arrow, bludgeoned, deprived of oxygen, electrocuted, throat slit with knife or with machinery, caught with hook or net," he checked himself to be sure he was in the right track by starring on faces for any negative reaction or caution. Finding no cautious reaction from no one, he continued.

"How does it really matter now if plants, vegetables, fruits and grains are chopped with knife, plucked, dug, grinded, juiced, bitten, chewed, drank, shushed, roasted, toasted, boiled, steamed, sautéed, cooked," he appeared worked-up but continued.

"Does it really matter now if you only eat seafood? Does it really matter if you eat both seafood and meats? Does it really matter if you do not eat seafood or meats at all? Animal Advocates, Vegetarians, Vegans, and all others should learn to live in harmony with each other. Live, and eat, and enjoy what the Creator has rightfully provided for everyone."

Shortly, they pulled into the driveway.

"We're home!" Ami exclaimed.

"Home indeed," Jeremiah echoed. "I'm overwhelmed with all phases of experiences today on this exceptional ride," he added.

"Me too especially at Walsh's Farm," Maxwell joined in.

"At least the truth had been told," Faith said as she got out of the vehicle.

The conversation would have continued and gained momentum outside the driveway had their mother not cut in.

"Let's get these stuffs inside" (referring to items bought at Walsh's)

Each person took turn removing items from the van to the house. The culture of the atmosphere in the house seemed normal as everyone is busy putting away bought food items where they belong until a generic question was asked:

"Who is hungry?" Dad threw question in the thin air.

"I'm starving," Maxwell quickly caught question with response.

"Let's got ready then to kill more plants Offspring," his dad *enlightened*.

"Dad you sound more and more aggressive in your approach to drive home your point," Maxwell observed.

"Listen my knowledge of biology describes Offspring as the end result of reproduction of a new organism produced by one or more parents - those are fruits, the seeds, of course baby animals too. So as you think animals, think plants too. Some people approach to life is so one sided like this statement I overheard made by someone during a conversation with another person, he began to paraphrase: I eventually became more concerned to the suffering of animals...to eat them without appropriate justification is immoral…I refused to be part of and to shoulder the responsibility for such horrible acts."

"You are so right dad because I heard this from my friend's mother: she had claimed she became a vegetarian because she felt terrible eating meat of animals…her reasons ended with a conclusive desire to put an end to animal suffering. Then a friend of my friend's mother side of the story was that, when she had a clear knowledge of what those helpless animals go through she completely switched to vegetarian diet. She also added, people absolutely don't have any right to kill these animals for their satisfaction, they're part of this planet earth as are people and that they should be able to live too, Maxwell exhaustively contributed."

"Faith I'm glad you just stepped in on time," Maxwell drawn the sister into this specific aspect of people reactions as to why they do not eat animals or why they became vegetarians etc. "What did you tell me your classmate said why he stopped eating meat from animals and dairy products?" he asked but pondered if it was his sister that told him that or from another source.

"His resolution was that he was against cruelty to animals and that the spiritual side of him prompted him to respect animal lives in particular and lives in general," Faith quickly participated with an answer to assured Maxwell she told him that.

"That's it, thank you dear sister; dad you heard that?" Maxwell looked at the father just to be sure he was listening and still in the conversation.

The father indicated in agreement with a nod. He however added, "like I said earlier, folks should learned to distinguished between feelings over reason," he then turned to concentrate on what he was doing but Maxwell begged for the father's pardon and attention so to shared one more unknown source of school of thought he read: It's disgusting to kill these living creatures and to eat them…not caring about the unbelievable mental and physical suffering of these creatures in the food industry, he paraphrased. As he was about to continue the doorbell rang.

"See who that is. It should be Sunny, I was expecting him," their father directed.

"Who is it?" Faith answered the door. She was closer to the door than the brother.

"It is uncle (paused) uncle Sunny," a voice answered from outside.

Sunny is Ami's close relative on the mother side of the family in Nigeria. Both reside in the same County here in the States about 7 miles radius from each other. He is visiting as they traditionally do from time to time checking on one another besides phone contacts and communications.

"Uncle," Faith happily and respectfully addressed Sunny as she welcomed him inside the house.

"Thank you Faith," Sunny greeted as he was being ushered to the kitchen where Maxwell and the father were putting a meal together.

"Mbakara," Ami greeted in his native dialect and shook hands with Sunny followed with a hug.

"Mbakara" means a White person and Sunny is teased as being White now that they resided and naturalized in "Whites" country.

"What's cooking?" Sunny teasingly asked.

"Some good stuff, welcome uncle Sunny," Maxwell proudly answered as he shook hands.

"Thanks Max! Wow! I've not seen you for quite a while," Sunny expressed gratitude.

"Your brother and mom home?" he inquired.

"Yes, upstairs. They should be down soon. We just got home not long ago," Maxwell explained. "I and dad are prepping these victims for meal," he added with a slight laugh.

"What victims are you referring to?" Sunny reacted curiously.

"The fruits, the veggies, the chickens, cows, sheep, pigs and the goats," a distinctive loud voice of Jeremiah rang as he descended the stairs heading towards the kitchen with smiles beaming on his face.

"Jeremiah," Sunny excitedly proclaimed and threw arms around Jeremiah as they both greeted each other.

"Uncle, welcome," Jeremiah responded as he broke away from the warm hug with Sunny.

By now, laughter from everyone filled the room in reaction to Jeremiah's style of declaring who the victims in question were as he joined in the kitchen. The atmosphere is so intense with admiration and the subject matter just introduced to Sunny. Faces are covered with smiles, alternating looks from one to another anticipating the next cue from among them.

"Here uncle, start with this," Faith present a tray with fruits and a glass of juice to Sunny who had taken seat at the eat-in dining table.

"Yea, that's your first set of victims according to my dad. Tell him dad if you did not do so yet," Maxwell joked picking up from where the brother left off.

"Thanks Faith, and you too Max," Sunny thanked both of them for the courtesy.

"Ehm," Sunny turned to Ami obviously about to ask him for explanation what the children were referring to as "victims" and of course the excitement and amusement looming around the subject matter.

"Don't bother to asked," Ami interrupted Sunny. "Question, are plants really Living Things?" He quickly began with a rhetorical question.

"I remember my study of Photosynthesis…" Sunny ignored the fact that the question was not solely directed on him to answer. However, Ami interrupted him.

"Hold your thought my brother," he indicated to Sunny. "Here is where more lights needed to be thrown. Some maintained plants are not living things because they don't breathe or move like humans and animals do. Some said they are Living Things yet are not alive with conscience like humans. That's conflicting, how can they be Living Things but not alive? Some said it is only the plants that are alive but not the fruits. As I said earlier, fruits are offspring - the end result of reproduction by most living organisms. You started saying something about Photosynthesis when I interrupted."

"Yes I said, I remembered my study of photosynthesis," Sunny resumed his lesson. "The term is used to describe the conversion of energy in living organisms. Photosynthesis is a very important chemical process for life. Light energy is converse into chemical energy in leaves cells (green pigment) called chlorophyll.

Through Photosynthesis, the sun's energy is made available to all organisms – plants, humans including animals. Humans depend on plants for oxygen. Conversely plants depend on humans for carbon dioxide. So humans, animals and plants respire (breathe) Let me break it down like this…:"

"Go ahead my brother," Ami encouraged.

"Say animal P (plant-eating animal) ate a plant. That animal P will get chemical energy from the plant just consumed. The said chemical energy was acquired by the plant through photosynthesis. Then came animal Y (that eats animal) and ate animal P. This animal Y will get some of the chemical energy animal P derived from eating the plant…"

"That my friend is the…" Ami interrupted Sunny but also got interrupted.

"Food chain, yes I remembered this from my biology class," Maxwell got involved. "The food chain is whereby groups of organisms are directly dependent on one another for food. My memory is back, the triangular-shaped-food chain otherwise known as Ecological Pyramid," Maxwell excitedly and imaginary drew in the air with his finger creating magnifying visual of the point he was attempting to make. All faces lit up with smiles as Maxwell used a funny voice to describe the imaginary picture he has drawn.

"I remembered this very clearly because it got me into trouble in the classroom for laughing so loud: my teacher had used Rabbit as the animal P that ate carrot and lettuce, in turn the Rabbit got eaten by an owl (animal Y) of which I made funny remarks that sparked laughter in the classroom."

"No, you didn't," Sunny sounded sarcastic. But Faith and the father nodded conclusively indicating to Sunny, yes Maxwell did. Smiles spread again on all faces.

"No doubts then, Vegetarians, Vegans, Carnivores, Herbivores, Omnivores, could substitute for animal P and or animal Y. Simply put it, people in general are Omnivores – both plants and animals eaters. However, the truth remained: whether you lived down or flew above; whether the organism lived or crawled on the ground, they depend on each other towards survival approach to staying alive," Ami reconciled.

"Ecologists look at the interrelationships amongst groups of organisms and their environments," Sunny elaborated on Ecological Pyramid raised by Maxwell. "For example, they look at the photosynthesis process in which plants and certain other organisms use the energy from the sun to convert carbon dioxide into glucose (sugar) and oxygen. Most importantly, plants produced their own food. They…"

"Are called, Primary Producers," Jeremiah emerged with an answer before Sunny completed. "Ooh! I feel like I'm in the classroom setting again," Jeremiah said with excitement.

"Then we (humans) subsequently eat the Primary Producers," Sunny submitted.

"No, we don't eat Primary Producers rather we preyed on them," Ami down played on the words. Everyone looked at him in reaction he said it that way.

"While plants are known as Primary Producers, we are the… Sunny got no chance to finish.

"Primary Consumers," all voices along with Sunny chorused an answer together.

"Then the Secondary Producers and Secondary Consumers followed the order. So yes my brother, plants are Living Things or Living Organisms," Sunny concluded the lecture in a nutshell.

"Thank you! Thank you!" Ami took a Chinese bow and proceeded with rhetorical summation.

"Is there an advocate group(s) for the sea foods or sea animals – fish, crabs, shellfish etcetera should not be killed and consumed; the graceful or less painful ways to kill or slaughter or cook them; besides checking how many particular sea food a person may catch in certain or allowable seasons; otherwise sizes of the sea food being catch at any given time as regulated by law; besides focus on or advocacy for proper labeling, sustainability and if blood of some specific, protected fish species has tainted other seafood. For instance, think or imagine live crabs thrown into a pot of boiling water over 100o closed in with lid so they cannot escape. Even if one of them was lucky enough, jumped out of the pot, would not got too far to escape its fate by the cruel hands of mankind. I am not advocating, but only showing the other side of life much noise is not heard," Ami ended painting the frightening pictures.

Uncontrollable laughter and part sympathy engulfed the room as each person took seat at the dining table at the eat-in kitchen.

"Faith, don't sit yet. Please call your mom to come so we could eat," her father asked.

"I'm here," Dieudonnée announced as she emerged coming down from upstairs steps.

"Madam Dee Dee," Sunny took pleasure to greet as he stood up both exchanging a warmth hugging.

"In-Law, Welcome! Your brother said you were coming," Dieudonnée responded. "How is your wife?" she asked.

"She is fine. Thank you! She is at work. You look good. I see evident of great care your husband has given to you," Sunny teased with a smile slightly looked at Inyang. Dieudonnée also returned a soft smile.

"May we pray," Ami closed his eyes but paused for his wife to take her seat which Sunny had slighted out for her. She padded Sunny on the shoulder for the courtesy. Ami began to bless the food as everyone joined hands. When he was done all confirmed with resounding… "Amen!"

While spoons, forks and knives were busy in the plates, Sunny seemed to have forgotten or left something out in his lecture and scientific clarification on plants being Living Things. He swiftly began:

"There are the trees, the grass, the herbs, the flowers, the fruits and many more. But they do not think or act or do as if they are persons with a mind or will. Rather, they are all under the control of their Creator who gave them lives – He called them all into Living Things and it was so – the Biblical creation story: "In the beginning God created the heavens and the earth. And the earth was without form and void…"

"That's Genesis 1:1-2," Dieudonnée named the book and the portions of the Bible.

"There is a verse or verses in Genesis 1 that directly addressed the creation of plants," Sunny pointed out, tried to remember the exact verse(s). He sat still, his head partially tilted with face facing up no doubt in deep thought.

"In-Law please eat, don't worry about that now," Dieu tried to broke his trend of thoughts.

"Don't strained your brain, excused me for a second," Ami said as he dashed to the desk at the Family Room adjacent to the Eat-in-Kitchen and grabbed a small Bible. He opened the Bible and immediately announced.

"Here, verses 11 and 12," he began to read starting with verse 11: "And God said, Let the earth bring forth grass, the herb yielding seed, and the fruit tree yielding fruit after his kind, whose seed is in itself, upon the earth: and it was so.

"Verse 12," he announced as he continued to read: 'And the earth brought forth grass, and herb yielding seed after his kind, and the tree yielding fruit, whose seed was in itself, after his kind: and God saw that it was good'. "May the Lord add blessings to the reading of His Words," Ami ended with profound joy all over his facial expression.

"Amen!" Everyone chorused with excitement.

"So, God called the world into being out of nothing. He created everything out of nothing," Sunny rested.

"Well noted! The fact is," Ami took the lead again. "Not all animal blood is red. The reason to that is lack of hemoglobin – a red pigment that gives the blood a red color. Take for example, the crabs (Living Things, from sea foods family) their blood is not red like that of fish but blue. They have blue pigment. They are invertebrates with jointed bodies. More so, they do not have blood vessels. If their skins are cracked they can bleed to death."

"Dad let's take another example," Maxwell followed. "The cockroaches (Living Things, also insects) they do not have respiratory pigment, therefore their blood is colorless. When they infest vegetarian and non- vegetarian homes they are ruthlessly slaughtered without any consideration to life like given to chickens and the rest of the animals by those groups who may care."

"I have another great example," Jeremiah joined in. "The annelids - like segmented worms (Living Things) they don't have green pigment or red pigment. That's why we hardly see their blood when rigged - the pointed hook and barb pushed into the delicate flimsy texture sacrificed for fish baits."

"Helpless worms, I feel for the poor fishes too that rushed for what they thought was genuine measures (food) to use for sustenance," Dieudonnée sounded sympathetic.

"A trap, deadly trap," Maxwell added laughing between lines. His laughter turned contagious – everyone caught it.

"So are the trees/plants (Living Things)" Sunny sounded on a serious note, they bleed sap - a mixture of water, starches, sugars and more, which the plants has absorbed from nutrients through its roots and leaves. When the plant realized it has been wounded, the chemicals in the sap change and clot at the spot the plant has been oozing the sap. The question again, do plants bleed? Sure they do. Bleeding in plants could be described as damage, a cut to a plant that causes sap (blood) to run from the wound. It's a simple experiment – step in your yard and break or cut your flower plant and observed the damaging results."

"Dad, remember the secretary at my doctor's office who shared with us how bad she felt when her flower plant died. She inadvertently had forgotten to water the plant and left it outside under the scourging sun. She discovered it withered the following day. She was so emotionally attached to the beautiful plant full of life but then died because of her negligent," Faith recollected.

"Yes, clearly remembered. I gave her credit for acknowledging the plant was alive before she killed it. That's what I called, respect for life, respect for all Living Things," her father gracefully responded. As they were eating, the father asked Faith if she wanted the ice cream that was served.

"I am a vegan," she blotted out. "No thanks for asking, I got my brand," she added more politely with a gleaming smile.

All eyes turned in her direction. Maxwell gave her a quirky smile.

"How was the meal?" Ami asked.

"Delicious!" Sunny took the lead to respond and compliment.

Maxwell mumbled a response with mouthful of ice cream. Everyone giggled in reaction. There was no doubt the food was enjoyed which means everything worked in harmony at the dinner table – the vegetarian (Faith) was satisfied, the meat consumers also satisfied.

Ami and Sunny relocated from the dining room to the living room to watch Nigerian News and events productions on Nigeria Television Authority (NTA). The children teamed up to cleaned the table and washed dishes while the mother headed to the family room to watch her favorite TV ministries. She was later joined by the children.

While Sunny and Ami were talking in the living room, a phone call interrupted their conversation. Ami excused himself to take the call. He returned and joined Sunny in about 7 minutes.

"Acquaintance," Ami notified Sunny.

They resumed where they were interrupted by the call and took the evening into the nightfall till 10:00 PM.

"I'm leaving," Sunny announced and bid everyone farewell after a fare time of relaxation and after the sumptuous meal and social interactions with the entire family. Each person in return took turn to bid farewell to Sunny and sent greetings to his wife. Ami walked with him outside to his car in the driveway.

"I am grateful you could come. Thanks!" Ami shook hands with Sunny and embraced with pats on the back.

"It could not be better than this especially tonight with all the educational inputs and contributions from the family to your ideology which allowed me the privilege to be part of. I am impressed," Sunny patted Ami on the shoulder.

He got in his car and waved as he drove off. Ami waved back and blew a kiss in the air with both hands.

It was 2:00 AM, the phone rang. Ami tiredly reached to answer the call. It had been his inner gratification and admiration to serve his congregants to the best of his ability. He actually encouraged them to call him anytime including nights (no matter how late) to share their personal predicaments, issues and especially for prayers. This was typical of such calls.

"Hello! Hello!" Ami's voice hardly faded as a desperate, scared, alarming chain reaction voice cried out.

"Rev, Rev, Rev, they're attacking me, they're after me... the plants...the trees. Help! Please help!" unidentified shaky voice prevailed.

"Walsh, is this you?" Ami probed. The sound of the voice at the other end got him fully awaken because of the frightening intensity of the caller.

"They're attacking me, help! Help me!" The caller continued wildly.

"Walsh, Walsh," Ami seemed to be sure whose voice he was dealing with.

Dieudonnée is woken by the husband's intense voice.

"What is it? Who is it? What's wrong? Something wrong?" she curiously and desperately probed. But the husband was not answering to any of the questions rather concentrated with Walsh due to the seriousness and state of affairs.

"Oh! My God, all are coming off at the roots from everywhere...help me. Please save me...they are throwing the fruits at me," Walsh vocalized louder but still not acknowledging to Ami, it was him on the line. However Ami did not bother to ask for identity at this point because he was fully convinced Walsh was the one on the line.

Remember Walsh was the farmer the Ami and wife patronized and shopped in his roadside farm kiosk. He was earlier accused by Ami of destroying and terminating plants lives without regards to life and guilt.

"Walsh calmed down," Ami launched for appealing solution. "It's Walsh, dear," Ami finally hinted the wife.

"Is he alright?" she enquired leaning closer to the husband in an attempt to picked Walsh's voice and what he may be saying to the husband. The husband got up on his feet from his sitting position on the edge of the bed.

Walsh just had a bizarre nightmare which transcended to reality that made him lose control and unable to took grip of his senses. It appeared he was literally in a trance, sleepwalking. He was being attacked by plants in general.

"It's a REVOLUTION!" He sounded confused in his utterances. "Tell them I won't kill them anymore," he seemed to be conversing with Rev at some point but suddenly made strange responses as to a third party…

"Please don't slapped again…why are all these trees surrounding me? Listen to me I won't destroy you like that any longer. I'm guilty, it is wrong to treat you all like you don't hold life," Walsh continued rambling on.

"Walsh let me pray with you," Rev Ami alerted. His wife stepped up and held his hand ready for an intersession prayer. Rather than a consenting voice for prayer, Ami heard another alarming cry...

"A tree trunk...huge trunk is rolling towards me. Oh no, it's not one but many of them descending down the hill. Stop them...I'm gonna be crushed."

"I rebuked them in the matchless name of Jesus Christ," Rev Ami launched with a commanding voice. "I rebuked them, I condemned, command the demonic power that is roaming around you now to depart in the Precious Powerful name of our Lord Jesus Christ. Every satanic attack destroyed. I cancelled the agenda of the evil messenger. I command the deceiving spirit of nightmare to disappear," he prayed with authority, his voice became stronger and he began to sweat.

"My Lord, my God, The Almighty Father, may every stronghold of Satan be broken. Please remove, erase Walsh's name from its books. Walsh, I plead and soaked you in the blood of Jesus our Savior. You are covered by His blood...protected by His power...I am coming after you devil with the Redeeming Power of the Lamb of God..."

"Amen!" Walsh voice resonated just before Rev could continue with another prayer point.

"Amen, Halleluiah!" Rev echoed with joy and more power.

"Say Amen!" Rev commanded and shouted.

"Amen!" Walsh obeyed.

"Say Amen!" Rev repeated.

"Amen!" Walsh responded.

"Shout, shout Glory!" Rev prompted.

"Glory, Glory!" Walsh followed.

"Don't stop, don't stop," Rev ordered.

"Glory, Glory, Glory, Halleluiah!" Walsh added.

"Yes Halleluiah, you're right, shout for your deliverance," Rev empowered.

Walsh must have evoked a strong feeling of emotional encounter and belief earlier with Ami and went to bed with that on his mind. The captivating experience and weighty thought carried him into this transient dream. It is quite a fundamental misunderstanding of how one may be affected by some degree of truth and reality. It is absolutely no doubt that Walsh took this revelation to heart.

Rev's phone suddenly signaled another incoming call while he was still on the line with Walsh.

"Excused me Walsh, I have another call just came in," Rev shared. "Stay positive and held on to your faith. I'll check on you in the morning. My prayer goes out continually on your behalf. Do not hesitate to call if you need to before morning broke," he encouraged and ended on affirmative note.

"Hello!" Ami paused for response.

"Who is it? What is it now?" Dieudonnée, his wife pressed with heightened curiosity even before her husband could get acknowledgement of who that could be.

"It's Eugenie!" the voice on the line identified in frightening tone.

"It's Eugenie," Ami whispered to Dieu his hand covering the phone.

"I'm being attacked by plants and vegetables in this weird dream," Eugenie shared. "It appeared they are revolting," she paused.

"It's a REVOLUTION," Ami whispered again to Dieu.

"Revolution," Dieudonnée strangely reacted with rhetorical and sympathetic response.

"Yes, revolution," Eugenie confirmed the echo she captured from Dieudonnée whispered response.

Eugenie is an acquaintance to the Ami's family. If you recollected the phone call Ami excused himself to answer while with Sunny in the living room, it was Eugenie who had called. During their remote conversation, Ami had told her in a nutshell what he had been up to during the day to include the stop family had made at Walsh Farm to deprivation of lives in plants by cooking them along with animal meat and eating them. She was another serious thinker that absorbed the theory to heart.

"Eugenie, we must pray. Don't forget the meaning of your name, Noble. You are noble to God. You are noble in God's eyes. He shall let no harm touched you. Disperse all appalling thoughts in your mind. Compose yourself, I'm here with you. Everything will be alright. I am a firm believer that prayers sure changes things. Do not entertain any doubts while God is at work. God is on your side. If God on your side, who can be against you. Let us pray," Rev fortified his self in another fervent prayer.

FIRING SQUAD

All lined up at firing range – objects of sacrifice to serve one purpose: sustained human appetite and livelihood. So let's eat freely, maintained healthy habits and Live peacefully and happily thereafter!

One year later Faith would have become a full vegetarian solely on Health Reasons